BILLIONAIRE BOSSMAN

A BEDDING THE BILLIONAIRE NOVELLA

LAURA LEE

This book is dedicated to all the strong women in the world who've been labeled a bitch because you don't take shit from anyone. You keep doin' you, girl!

CHAPTER ONE

AVERY

"Oh yeah, give it to me, Big Daddy!"

"I'll give it to you, baby. I'll give it to you real good."

What in the actual fuck?

I'm home a day early from my business trip to surprise my fiancé, Stuart. Considering it's three in the afternoon on a Wednesday, said fiancé should be in the office reviewing the contract that I had signed, sealed, and delivered into his lap after spending the last two days in Atlanta. What he should *not* be doing, is banging his secretary over the back of our couch.

Neither one of them have noticed me at this point, so I watch with morbid fascination as he ruts into her like a pig in heat. I don't really know what pigs look like when they mate but comparing him to swine seems rather appropriate at the moment, don't you think?

"Oh, Stewie, just like that! Your cock is so huge I can barely take it!"

Huge? The only way *Stewie* would be considered huge is if you were comparing him to a gherkin. Even then, it's a toss-up.

Stuart grabs her hips and starts doing his best impression of a jackhammer. "Uh...Callie...baby, you're so fucking tight. I'm not going to last much longer."

Hate to break this to you, *Callie baby*, but Stuart *never* lasts much longer. I look at the face of my Rolex—the watch he just gave me for my twenty-ninth birthday—and think to myself that this will be over in about a minute.

A vein pops in the middle of Stuart's forehead as he throws his head back. "Unh...yeah, that's it. I'm coming, baby! I'm coming so hard!"

Okay...so it was more like ten seconds.

"Mmm, yeah, baby, I'm coming too. Ooh, yeah, give it to me." Callista's voice is slightly porny, which leads me to believe that she's totally faking it.

Been there, honey.

You're probably wondering why I haven't said anything at this point, right? I should be spitting mad. Ready to take a stand on behalf of all women scorned. Maybe I should be yelling or throwing things, or at the very least, let them know that I'm standing in the doorway so they'd put an end to this shit show. I'd be lying if I said the thought of chucking my Louboutins at his face didn't sound appealing, but truthfully, Stuart Reed is not worth potentially breaking a heel.

In fact, these two are doing me a favor. Stuart and I have been together since college, but our relationship has been dead for a long time. I don't even know why I agreed to marry him in the first place. It just seemed like a natural progression since we had been a couple for so many years. We got along well, and we had similar interests, so it made sense, I guess. Sex between us was always lackluster at best, but I'm not really one of those women that prioritizes bedroom activities. Sure, it's nice to have a release sometimes, but my showerhead can do that for me just fine.

I never understood that all-consuming desire that you see in movies or read about in romance novels, where people can't keep their hands off each other. Quite frankly, I think the whole concept is asinine. I get much more satisfaction out of signing a big client than I've ever had from a lover.

I cross my arms over my chest as their bodies fall lax and then I clear my throat. "Hi, guys. How's it going?"

Their eyes widen comically as they disentangle from one another. Callista shrieks and starts gathering her clothing off the floor while Stuart remains frozen in shock, with his pants around his ankles.

"A-Avery," he stutters. "What are you doing here? You're not supposed to be back until tomorrow."

I arch an eyebrow and nod toward the couch. "Yeah, Stuart, it's pretty damn obvious you weren't expecting me."

He quickly looks at his secretary and back to me again. "Darling, this isn't what it looks like. It didn't mean anything."

I don't miss the glare Callista sends his way. She remains mute though, and makes a run for it after she finishes dressing.

"I'm so sorry, Avery," she whispers as she passes me.

I scoff. "Yeah, I bet."

Stuart pulls his pants up and steps toward me.

I hold my hand up to ward off his advance. "If

you'd like to keep your nuts intact, you probably shouldn't get any closer, Stuart."

He blanches. "Avery, I swear, this was a one-time thing."

"Really?" I challenge. "So that's supposed to make it better? Why was she even in our apartment, Stuart?"

He gulps. "I decided to work from home today, and she was dropping off contracts. Callie's been coming on to me for a while, and you and I haven't made love in months and well...I'm a man. I have needs."

"Wow...so let me get this straight. This is *my* fault?"

He shakes his head. "No, sweetheart, that's not what I was saying. I messed up. I swear it won't happen again."

"Oh. Okay then."

He blinks rapidly. "Really? You're okay with this?"

I roll my eyes. "No, I'm not okay with this, you moron! You were just fucking your secretary over the back of our couch. How would that *ever* be okay?"

He pinches the bridge of his nose as if I'm the unreasonable one. "Look, Avery, we need to find a way to get past this. I'll buy another couch if that helps. We can forget this little...incident ever happened. There's too much at stake at the firm to allow a silly personal issue to affect our productivity. There's no I in team, Aves. We need each other."

Sadly, he's right about our working relationship. In that respect, Stuart and I burn hotter than ever. We're the top closers by a mile at one of the largest PR firms in New York. A firm that Stuart's father just happens to own, but nothing was handed to us —we've earned our status through talent, long hours, and drive. Our client list contains actors, athletes, supermodels, and the occasional mogul or Wall Street douchebag. Together, we've brought in over a hundred million dollars to Reed & Associates in the past year alone.

I narrow my eyes. "You should've thought about that before you stuck your dick inside your secretary."

He throws his hands up in exasperation. "I said it wouldn't happen again!"

I pick my bag up off the floor. "You're right, Stuart. It won't because I'm done. I'll be at a hotel until I can make other arrangements. Don't worry; I'll send you the bill. It'd be great if you can be gone tomorrow so I can come to get my things."

"You can't be serious! You're just going to throw away the last seven years of our lives?"

"Oh, I'm serious," I confirm. "We may have to work together, but we don't have to *be* together. I can be professional in the office, and I hope you can do the same." I pry my engagement ring off my finger and set it on the entry table. "I hope *Callie baby* keeps your tiny dick happy."

His jaw drops. "Tiny?! I'll have you know it's perfectly average. Above average, maybe." He narrows his eyes. "Maybe you're too loose from all the men you've slept with. Ever think about that?"

I roll my eyes. He and I both know that I've only been with two other men. Also, I'm a Kegel master. "You keep telling yourself that, Stewie. Your teeny wienie isn't my problem anymore. If you wanted it tighter, you should've brought a bigger dick to the table."

I don't give him a chance to reply before I walk out the door and slam it behind me. Unsurprisingly, he doesn't even attempt to follow, probably still pouting over my insult to his manhood. It may have been a cheap shot on my behalf, but the look on his face when I said it makes me smile during the entire elevator ride down to the lobby.

CHAPTER TWO

2 MONTHS LATER

AVERY

My secretary, Diane, stands up, wringing her hands the moment I walk into the office. Why the hell does she look so nervous?

"Ms. Jacobs, Mr. Reed would like to see you in his office immediately."

I sigh. "*Which* Mr. Reed?"

"Senior, ma'am."

Great. This is the last thing I need today. I'm so far behind on everything because Stuart refuses to act like a goddamn professional and pull his weight. We broke up two months ago and yet every day, he spends his time begging me to take him back instead of actually working. And every day, I tell him I'd rather eat dog shit than ever have his microscopic dick inside of me again.

"Thank you, Diane. Will you let him know I'll be right up?"

She nods. "Yes, ma'am."

I drop my purse in my office and take the stairs up to the next floor. As I'm leaving the stairwell, the elevator dings and the doors open. Stuart's standing inside, with his hand wrapped around Callista's hip.

He gives me an arrogant smirk before placing a kiss on her lips. "I'll be back down as soon as I take care of this and we can resume our *conversation*."

She squeals as he pinches her ass. "Okay, baby. I can't wait."

I ignore them and start walking down the hallway toward Stuart Sr.'s office. When Stuart Jr. catches up to me, I give him the side-eye. "Does that little show mean that I can finally count on you leaving me the fuck alone?"

Stuart straightens his tie. "Oh, you can count on a lot of things, Aves. One of which is that you're about to be standing in the unemployment line."

I glare at him. "What the hell are you talking about?"

He knocks twice on his father's office door. "You're about to find out."

"Come in," Mr. Reed says.

I step tentatively into his father's office, still trying to figure out why his son has to be here, too. "You wanted to see me, sir?"

Mr. Reed nods to the chairs in front of his desk. "Yes, please sit down. Both of you."

I make a point to scoot my chair over a few inches before taking a seat beside my asshole ex. "Sir, with all due respect, my workload is really heavy right now, so if we could make this as quick as possible, I'd appreciate it."

Mr. Reed removes his glasses and places them in front of him. "Yes, Avery. Well, that's what I wanted to talk to you about. Your work."

"What about it?"

He nods to his son. "Well, to be frank, my son has brought some alarming issues to my attention."

I raise my eyebrows. "Such as?"

Out of the corner of my eye, I see Stuart grinning. *Oh, this is going to be interesting.*

Stu Sr. clears his throat. "That you haven't been contributing to your shared accounts. That he's been having to put in extra hours each week because you've refused to cooperate with him since your relationship ended. The most concerning is that you've broken our no fraternization policy with one of our highest grossing clients."

I bolt out of my chair. "Are you kidding me?!" I look around for hidden cameras. "Is this a joke?"

Mr. Reed frowns. "I assure you, Ms. Jacobs, this is no laughing matter. Now, please sit back down."

I remain standing and shoot Stuart what I hope is my best ball-shriveling glare. "Our highest grossing client is a seventy-six-year-old media mogul who should buy stock in Viagra, considering how many bimbos he has on rotation. Why on earth would you think I'd like to join his harem?"

Stuart Jr. scoffs. "*I saw you, Avery.* He had you pressed against his limo, shoving his tongue down your throat on the corner of 86th and Lexington. Is that why you broke up with me? Because you're looking for a sugar daddy?"

My jaw drops and for a moment, I'm incapable of speaking. I can't believe he actually has the nerve to pull this shit! After all these years together, how could he do something so vicious? Especially when he's the reason we split!

"I broke up with you, Stuart, because you're a lying, cheating asshole!"

Stuart Sr. stands. "Avery, there's no need for this outburst. Please, sit down."

"Oh, so now I'm Avery again?" I throw my hands up in exasperation. "Your son's accusations are one-hundred-percent false. For the record, *he* has been the one leaving *me* with an abundance of work because he refuses to be a goddamn professional."

"If that were true, why haven't you said anything up to this point?" Mr. Reed challenges. "Stuart brought his concerns about your work ethic to me *two months* ago. I've been giving you time to get your act together because you have been so valuable to Reed & Associates, but with this newest development, I could no longer keep silent."

I roll my lips, choosing my words carefully. "Because I'm a professional, and I'm more than capable of handling it. I've been the main point of contact for every one of our clients since they've signed with us. My work ethic has *never* been a problem. I log more hours than anyone in this building!"

Mr. Reed raises his eyebrows. "Are you accusing my son of lying?"

"Yes!"

Stuart laughs. "Please, Avery. There's no need to get nasty just because you've been caught. I can't help but wonder how many other clients you've bedded to get them to sign with us. Is that why you were never in the mood? Because you were too exhausted from giving it up all over town?"

I can feel my face reddening. "How dare you!"

Mr. Reed holds his hand up. "Stuart, Avery, we're not here to discuss your personal relationship. Whatever your reasons were for ending it, I don't care. What I *do* care about is the reputation of my business and how my employees conduct them-selves." He turns toward me. "And you, Ms. Jacobs, have violated one of our cardinal rules. I will not put this company at risk by continuing to employ you. If you leave quietly, I'll be sure to sweep this indiscretion under the rug and say you resigned so it won't affect your ability to stay in the PR indus-try. I do, however, highly recommend you recon-sider having personal relations with clients in the future."

"I don't believe this," I sneer. "Have you even talked to Mr. Shoemaker? Have you asked him if he had his elderly tongue down my throat?"

"Our employee policies are not his concern," he replies. "Stuart's word is good enough for me. Why would he lie about this? You've been a great team until recently."

I cross my arms over my chest. "Because he's a spineless, petty piece of shit?"

"Ms. Jacobs, there's no need for name calling," he admonishes.

"Oh, but trying to destroy someone's career is okay?"

Stuart's father straightens his tie, in the same haughty way his son did earlier. "Phil from security is waiting for you downstairs. You have one hour to clean out your office before I rescind my offer of keeping this between the three of us. Phil's been instructed to ensure you don't take any proprietary information with you, so don't bother attempting to do so. You can leave your keys and access badge with him."

"So, that's it? There's nothing I can do to challenge this?"

Mr. Reed scowls. "Ms. Jacobs, as you know, this is a privately held company. I do not have shareholders or a board to report to. My decision overrides anything else."

"We'll see what my attorney has to say about that."

He smirks. "Think long and hard before you go down that road, Avery. You and I both know how ruthless our legal team can be. If you ever want to work in PR again, I'd suggest keeping your name out of the press. You know how these things go; the truth doesn't matter. Perception does."

The fucking bastard is right. Bad press for a publicist would be career suicide.

"Best of luck, Aves." Stuart Jr. gives me a little finger wave.

"Fuck you, Stuart." I turn back toward his father. "And fuck you, too. I'm glad I didn't make the mistake of marrying into this family. You're both misogynistic assholes who clearly have no conscience."

Mr. Reed returns my glare. "One hour. You can see yourself out."

I leave the room with a two-finger salute and a promise to myself to never get involved with a co-worker again.

CHAPTER THREE

AVERY

"Fuck Reed & Associates!" my bestie, Heather, shouts. "You don't need them."

"Well, what I do need is a paycheck if you'd ever like me to get out of your spare bedroom."

She grabs the pint of Chunky Monkey from my hand and takes a bite. "I already told you that you're welcome here as long as you'd like. It's been fun having you as a roomie."

"No offense, babe, but I'm too old to have a roommate."

"Not in New York," she argues. "Especially Manhattan. Hell, I went out with a guy last week who's still living with his parents at thirty-three.

That's a little weird, but a roommate is nothing to be ashamed of."

"I'm not ashamed," I assure her. "I'd just like to have a place of my own."

"Why?"

"For one, I've never lived alone. I went from my parents' house to a dorm, to my apartment with Stuart." I look around her living room and gesture to the framed picture of Thor. "And two, you and I have very different tastes in home décor."

Heather laughs. "Chris Hemsworth's body *is* a work of art. No woman on this planet could deny that. That poster is far better than any Rembrandt."

Okay, I'll give her that. "And the *Funko Pop!* collection?"

She shrugs. "Those babies are an investment. Do you have any idea how much that bronze Ken Griffey Jr. is going for these days?"

I give her a wry look. "*They're toys*. Besides, I remember you saying the same thing about Furbies. And Beanie Babies."

She points her spoon at me. "Also an investment. If you don't believe me, check eBay. People pay up the ass for the rare ones."

"Yeah, people who have nothing better to spend their money on," I mutter.

She rolls her eyes. "Regardless, my point was that you have time to find a new job. You said you have some money saved up and you have a roof over your head. I'm sure you'll find a new position at an even better firm. You're Avery-fucking-Jacobs. Your reputation speaks for itself."

I sigh. "I hope so. Who knows what Stuart is saying about me? Public relations is a much smaller world than you might think."

"Stuart is a douchebag with a pencil dick. Like anyone would believe his word over yours."

"His father did."

"That's because his father is the original small-dicked douche. You have to forget about them, Avery. You know what I think you should do?"

This should be interesting. "What should I do, O' Wise One?"

"You need to get laid," she says matter-of-factly. "By someone with a huge cock."

My eyebrows lift. "And how do you suppose I do that? Take out an ad requesting dick pics?"

Heather shakes her head. "No, smartass. Go to a club. Flirt with a hot man. Go home with him, fuck like animals, and leave afterward. No real names. No phone numbers."

"You want me to have a one-night stand?"

"Why not? You're a twenty-nine-year-old, single, gorgeous woman living in New York City. You need to hit the reset button on your life, and this is the perfect way to do that."

"I don't know, Heath. I've never really been comfortable with the whole one-night-stand thing. I don't think there's anything wrong with them; they're just not for me."

"That's exactly why you need to do it!" she argues. "Trust me; there's nothing better to help get your mojo back than a good pounding from a hot guy. Even better if he knows how to eat pussy, since Stuart had no fucking clue."

I grab the ice cream back from her and take a huge bite. "Okay, let's pretend I'm on board with your plan. What if I find an attractive man that I'd like to go home with but when the pants come off, his goods are underwhelming?"

She smirks. "Trust me, Ave, if you can't tell he's packing while you're grinding up against him on a dance floor, throw him back into the sea. Fast."

I laugh. "Good point."

"So when are we doing this?" she asks. "Does tomorrow work for you?"

"Tomorrow is Thursday."

"So?" Heather shrugs. "This is New York City. Every night is a good night to go out, have a few drinks, and find someone to hook up with."

I sigh. "I'll probably regret this, but fine. Tomorrow it is."

CHAPTER FOUR

LIAM

"We've arrived, Mr. Maxwell."

"Thanks, Brent. I'll text you when I'm ready for a pickup."

His eyes meet mine in the rearview. "Yes, sir."

I exit my town car and step right past the line of people waiting to get into one of New York's hottest clubs, *Blanc*.

The security guard opens the velvet rope, allowing me to pass. "Good evening, Mr. Maxwell. Will anyone else be joining your party tonight?"

I extend my hand. "Not tonight, Frank. Although, if all goes well, I'll be leaving with someone."

He laughs. "Something tells me you won't have any problems with that, sir."

I smile. "I never do."

I head over to the VIP section, but I freeze as I glance to my left and spot the most magnificent creature on the dance floor. She's grinding against some blonde, putting on quite the show for every man in the vicinity. Her friend is cute, but she is absolutely *stunning*. Dark hair that falls to her waist in soft waves, pouty red lips that are perfect for sucking cock, and eyes so light they have an ethereal quality to them. And let's not forget about those mile-long legs or the more-than-a-handful tits that are spilling out of her tight black dress. She's hands down, the sexiest woman I've ever seen in my life.

I order a couple of drinks, watching her the entire time. I can't quite get a read on her, which is unusual for me. I can tell she's not exactly in her element here. There's something...*off* about her. Yet, she's all smiles and loose limbs as if she's having the time of her life. She and her friend finally leave the dance floor and enjoy a few drinks of their own, fending off the occasional douche that approaches their table.

I check my watch and see that it's already eleven o'clock. I have an early meeting tomorrow, so if I want to spend the next few hours between this beautiful woman's thighs, I need to make my move now.

Mark my words: She'll be screaming my name by midnight.

CHAPTER FIVE

AVERY

Heather nods to something over my shoulder. "Avery, that hottie in the black suit is staring at you again."

I discreetly turn in my chair so I can follow her gaze. Sure enough, the most gorgeous man that I've ever seen catches my eye. I bite my lip as I watch him take a sip of his drink, never breaking our connection. My nipples harden as he swallows the amber liquid and licks a stray drop from his lip. Since when is swallowing sexy? I've never had such a visceral reaction to a man before. I'm honestly not quite sure how to handle it.

"Go talk to him, Ave. He's obviously into you."

I turn back to her. "If that were the case, don't

you think he would've approached me by now? It's been well over an hour since we first saw him."

Her lips twitch. "Hold that thought while I hit the ladies' room."

"Do you want me to go with you?"

Heather stands up and grabs her little clutch purse off the table. "Nope. You stay *right here*."

I chuckle. "Okay, weirdo."

She winks. "Get him, girl."

Huh? I'm just about to follow her to ask what she meant, but I stop dead in my tracks as Mr. Black Suit approaches my booth.

He nods to the space that Heather had just vacated. "May I?"

"Uh...sure." God, I'm so out of practice with this. I work in communications for Christ's sake. I should be able to get through a simple conversation without sounding like an idiot.

Instead of sitting across from me like Heather was, he slides in right next to me, forcing me to scoot over.

"You don't mind, do you? It's quite loud in here, and I'd rather not shout across a table to speak with you."

"Uh...no...I guess not." Dammit, Avery, get your shit together!

Mr. Suit nods to my glass of wine. "May I get you another?"

I take a long sip to calm my nerves before answering. "No, thank you. This is actually my third glass. I should probably stop after this."

"I agree," he says. "I don't fuck drunk women."

"Um..." For probably the first time in my life, I'm absolutely speechless. I've been hit on many times in my life, but never, *ever*, has a man taken such a direct approach with me before. I start to take another drink of my wine, but he wraps his long fingers around the stem of the glass, stopping me.

Together, we set the goblet back on the table, but he doesn't release my hand. "What's your name?"

"A...Angela," I lie.

"A Angela?" His tone says he knows I'm giving him a fake name.

My face warms in embarrassment. "Just Angela."

His fingers move to my cheek before brushing a loose piece of hair behind my ear. "Well, *just Angela*, I'm Max."

I gulp. "It's nice to meet you, Max."

His whiskey-colored eyes twinkle as they look

me over with appreciation, pausing briefly on my cleavage before settling on my lips. "You've never been here before."

There's no question in his voice, so I merely shrug.

"Why not?"

"Clubs aren't really my thing." Unless I'm dragging a client out of one, saving them from becoming the next gossip headline.

Max raises an eyebrow with a sexy smile. "So why now?"

"It was my friend's idea. I recently got out of a relationship. She thought I needed...a night out."

"A night out?" He moves a bit closer. "Is that all?"

I stare at him as he stares back at me, not saying a word. God, I could look at this man all day long. He's so damn attractive, and he knows it. Max's jet black suit is perfectly tailored, hugging his body so well, that it leaves no doubt he's built beneath the fabric. His dark brown hair is purposely messy, in that freshly fucked kind of way. Hell, for all I know, he *is* freshly fucked.

This man carries himself with an arrogance that would usually send me running for the hills but instead, my body is begging me to sleep with him.

Although I have a sneaking suspicion there would be no actual *sleeping* going on.

His wolfish grin tells me that my thoughts are horribly transparent. "Are you going to answer my question, Angela?"

I blink, trying to remember what he asked. "Which question was that?"

He lets out a low laugh and leans into my ear. "Are you here for a simple night out with your friend...or were you looking for something else? Perhaps some*one* else?"

My nipples pebble as his deep voice rumbles against my earlobe. Since my dress is backless and wouldn't allow for a bra, if Max looks down right now, he'll know exactly how much he's affecting me.

"Could you elaborate on that?"

He rubs his nose against my cheek. "I'd *love* to. I was asking if you'd like to leave here with me so I can eat your pussy until you scream my name, dripping your sweet juices all over my chin. If you want me to fuck you with my nine-inch cock so hard, you would feel me for days afterward. If you'd beg me to *keep* fucking you until you couldn't see straight. Would you like that, *Angela*?"

"I—" Shit, panties would be really nice right

now. I'm pretty sure I'm leaving a wet spot on the leather bench.

Max licks a trail up my neck before biting my earlobe. "What's it going to be? It's a yes or no question."

"I—" God, what is taking Heather so long? I can't think straight around this man.

He pulls back with a twinkle in his eyes. "Text your friend and tell her you're leaving. I have a room at the Four Seasons. I'll have my driver take us."

"I—"

I still can't seem to spit any words out, so I take a sip of wine. This time, Max doesn't stop me. He simply waits me out as I finish the entire glass. Heather is still not back from the bathroom which leads me to believe she's not coming back. I retrieve my phone from my purse, and sure enough, there's an incoming text from her, telling me to have fun with the hot stranger.

I clear my throat. "I have a few rules."

"Go on."

"Well, first of all, this is just sex. I'm not looking for a relationship."

"Neither am I. Next?"

"Second, I don't want anything beyond tonight

—even if it's just physical. You can't have my phone number or my address."

Max's eyes dance with amusement. "Did I miss the part where I asked for either of those things?"

God, his cockiness should be a huge turn-off, but it's not. It makes me want to find out firsthand whether or not his cock really is nine inches.

"Third, you have to wear a condom. That's non-negotiable."

He nods. "That's fair. Any others?"

I bite my lip as I think about it for a few seconds. "No, I guess that's it."

He smiles and pulls his phone out of the coat's inner pocket. "Brent, I'm ready to head out. I have a friend with me. We'll be heading to the Four Seasons." Max ends the call after some more words and stands. "He'll be here in a few minutes. Are you ready?"

My thumbs fly over the screen of my phone as I text Heather, telling her where we're going. When I look up, Max is offering his hand, so I take it and slide out of the booth.

He leads me out of the club through a side entrance, where a black town car is waiting. Max follows me into the back seat and shuts the door.

"All set, sir?" the driver asks.

"Yes, Brent, we're good to go." Max rolls up the partition the moment his sentence is finished.

I can feel his eyes on me as the car pulls onto the busy Manhattan streets.

"So...the Four Seasons, huh? Are you in town for business?"

Max smiles as I turn toward him. "You could say that."

"What is it that you do?" I nervously play with the thin silver chain hanging from my neck. God, why am I so anxious? I'm normally a confident woman; you have to be in my field. But this guy throws me off kilter.

He places his hand on my bare knee and gives me a predatory grin. "Do you really want to know that...*Angela*?"

"No, I suppose I don't."

Before I can say another word, Max is pushing me down against the leather seat, shoving his tongue into my mouth. I close my eyes against the assault and allow my other senses to take over. Every brush of his fingertips as they slide higher and higher, the pillowy softness of his lips as they move against mine. I find myself wondering why no one has ever kissed me like this before. Why no one has been able to ignite this fire that is blazing inside of me. His kiss is pure domination, dripping with promises of what's to come.

I moan as I feel his hardened length against my thigh. Praise Jesus, this guy is definitely packing. I gasp when he palms my breasts through my dress, brushing his thumbs over my nipples.

When the car finally comes to a stop, I'm so lost in the moment, Max needs to pry my fingers out of his hair. We take a minute to adjust our clothing—and so he can adjust his hard-on—before exiting the vehicle.

The elevator ride to the fifteenth floor seems to be the longest elevator ride in existence. He removes a keycard from his wallet as we reach his room, and presses it against the panel until the light turns green. The second we're inside, and the door is closed, all bets are off.

Max shoves me against the wall and attacks my mouth. He fumbles with the hidden zipper on the side of my dress while he continues controlling our kiss. He pushes the straps off my shoulders as soon as my dress is unzipped, causing it to pool around my ankles. I'm now completely naked—except for my five-inch heels—and he's completely clothed. I reach for his belt buckle, but he steps back before I have a chance to grab it.

He rubs his trimmed beard as his eyes burn a path from my head to my toes and back up again. "Fuck, I don't know where I want to start first."

I lunge for his belt again. "How about getting undressed?"

His brown eyes turn molten as he seemingly decides what to do with me. "In a minute. First, I need to do this."

"Do wha—"

I squeal as Max suddenly lifts me over his shoulder and carries me across the room. Before I can ask him where we're going, he tosses me onto the bed and pulls me by the ankles until my knees are hooked over his shoulders. With no hesitation whatsoever, he dives into my pussy and sucks my clit into his mouth.

"Ah...oh fuck!" I cry out. "Shit...fuck...hold up a sec!"

"Why?" he murmurs into my slick flesh.

"Ah...um..."

I can't seem to form a sentence as his tongue makes slow, torturous circles. Holy shit, this man knows how to eat pussy. The entire time Stuart and I were together, he would only go down on me every once in a blue moon, and never gave much of an effort. It seemed like a chore to him. Not this man. He could teach a goddamn master's class on this shit, and he obviously enjoys it.

My toes curl when Max resumes his task, making me forget I even had an objection in the first place. Hell, he makes me forget my own name —the real one and my alter ego. I decide to take Heather's advice and just go with the flow. One night of incredible sex with this man will definitely help me get my mojo back.

CHAPTER SIX

LIAM

"Liam, did you hear anything I just said?"

I glance to my right and find my best friend and COO, Nick Sutton, flashing me a look of annoyance. Probably because I've been replaying my night with the gorgeous brunette instead of listening to him.

I kick my feet up onto the edge of his desk. He glares at the offending Ferragamos but wisely says nothing, considering I own the company.

"Sorry, I didn't get much sleep last night." Or *any* sleep. "What were you saying?"

He takes a deep breath. "I said, I think we found our candidate for the L.A. office."

"Let me see the resume."

Nick smiles. "I don't technically have one. Yet. But word on the street says that Avery Jacobs just left Reed & Associates."

I raise an eyebrow. "No shit?"

Avery Jacobs is a PR prodigy. I've wanted her on my team since the moment she showed up on my radar a few years ago. That woman could make a serial killer look like a saint. Much to my dismay, she's won over several of our clients when their contracts were up for renewal. I can't really blame them though. I'd want her to represent me, too.

"No shit. Left for personal reasons." He uses air quotes on the last two words then links his hands together behind his head. "Apparently, Reed Jr. was boinking his secretary, so she dumped him. If I had to guess, I'd say she can no longer handle working with that tool."

"I can't stand that guy. He's such a pompous ass. His father, too."

Nick belts out a laugh that would make you think I'm doing stand-up here. "Takes one to know one, huh?"

I roll my eyes. "Anyway...what do you suggest?"

He slides an employment contract across the desk. The terms are standard for the most part, but the salary and benefits he's proposing are well out of our norm.

"You want to offer a $350,000 salary? *Plus* moving expenses, a company car, and the condo in Beverly Hills? Are you fucking crazy?"

He leans forward and looks me in the eye. "We'd be asking her to move to the opposite end of the country. The housing is only temporary until she can find something on her own. And with as much money as she brought to that dickbag's company, three-fifty is nothing. We need to offer something she can't refuse. She's worth it, Liam. You know that."

You have no idea. The woman can fuck like a porn star.

Oh, did I forget to mention that Avery Jacobs is the hot brunette from last night? Yes, I knew exactly who she was when I approached her. The PR world isn't very big. In fact, I'm a little insulted she didn't recognize me. I'll give her a pass, though, since I'm only occasionally in New York these days and I can't even remember the last time I made a press statement. Why would I, when I have people to do that for me? Avery may not know who truly gave her the best dicking of her life, but she's about to.

I tap his desk with my knuckles. "Make the offer."

Nick smiles. "All right. I'll reach out to her today. Give me a call when your flight lands and I'll let you know how it goes."

CHAPTER SEVEN

1 MONTH LATER

AVERY

"I can't believe you're leaving me," Heather whines.

I squeeze her a little bit tighter before pulling away. "I know, honey, but we'll still talk all the time. It's scary for me, too; I've been in New York my entire adult life. But I couldn't pass on this opportunity. And besides, you know you'll be dying to come to visit me as soon as it starts snowing here."

She laughs. "True. Maybe by then, you'll have found yourself a hot surfer dude with hot surfer dude friends."

I smirk. "I'll see what I can do."

"Lady, you coming, or what?" the cab driver asks.

I throw my carry-on bag into the backseat. "Yep. Just give me a few more seconds." I grab Heather and hold on tightly just once more. "I'll call you as soon as I get to my new home."

She has tears in her eyes. "Okay. Facetime so you can show me your apartment. Love you."

"Love you, too." I wave to her through the back window as the car drives away.

When Maxwell & Company offered me a position as the Director of Public Relations for their L.A. office, at first, I thought someone was playing a joke on me. It seemed too good to be true. Once I realized it was legit, I signed on that dotted line immediately, before they had the chance to rescind their offer. Who in their right mind could turn down a higher level position, a *huge* pay raise, plus several amazing perks?

One of the biggest draws is that my new company has two offices—one in New York and the other in L.A.—and they each have their own specialty. The Los Angeles firm manages clients who work in the entertainment industry. The New York office handles the moguls and large corporations, which to be frank, I won't miss one bit. While I've had my fair share of drama with actors, damage control is usually pretty easy since acting is what they do for a living. I tell them what role they need to play in the public eye, and they do it. Pretentious businessmen, not so much.

As the cab pulls up to JFK International, I smile, thinking about the possibilities that lie ahead. This is my chance to start fresh. I'll have new clients in a new city. I'll get to make new friends and discover which places have the best take out. And the greatest perk of all? I won't have to walk into an office every day and face an asshole who's seen me naked.

CHAPTER EIGHT

LIAM

Over the last ten years, Maxwell & Company has gone from a boutique startup to a critical player in the PR industry. In the beginning, I was the face of the company, but Nick assumed that role about five years ago when I opened the L.A. office. He still runs all significant decisions by me, but I no longer deal with the bullshit minutiae that running a multi-billion dollar company entails. It's probably the only reason Avery Jacobs has no idea who she's truly working for.

Speaking of Avery, today's her first day on the job. The entrepreneur in me can't wait to get her up and running. I can practically see the money rolling in. Unfortunately, the male side of me also can't wait to bring her onboard.

I haven't been able to get her off my mind since that night over four weeks ago. I don't know why; repeats aren't usually my thing, no matter how well they suck dick. But sadly for said dick, I don't dip my pen in the company ink. No matter how fantastic she is in the sack, it's not worth the potential fallout.

I hit the speaker button when my desk phone buzzes, "Mr. Maxwell, Ms. Jacobs is just finishing with Human Resources. Shall I have them send her here?"

"Yes, that'd be great, Olivia. And you're free to take lunch as soon as you show her in."

"Thank you, sir," she says.

I rise from my custom-built mahogany desk and button my coat. As they say in the entertainment biz, it's showtime.

CHAPTER NINE

AVERY

As I approach my new boss's office, a gorgeous blonde is waiting in the antechamber. She smiles warmly as she approaches me.

"Ms. Jacobs?"

I shake the hand she's offering. "Please, call me Avery."

"It's nice to meet you, Avery. I'm Olivia, Mr. Maxwell's assistant."

"It's nice to meet you as well." I nod to the closed door. "He wanted to see me?"

"He's expecting you. You can go right in." Before I can place my hand on the doorknob, she adds, "Don't let him intimidate you." Her voice is quiet, barely more than a whisper.

I tilt my head to the side and match her volume. "Pardon me?"

Olivia waves her hand toward his office. "He can be a bit of an...well, *difficult* at times. Although in the end, his bark is worse than his bite. A word of advice though—woman to woman—he's insanely good-looking, and he knows it. Don't let that distract you because he *will* call you out on it, and it won't be pleasant."

"I'll keep that in mind," I say, finding myself equal parts grateful for the warning, yet disturbed by her unprofessionalism.

I paste a smile on my face and step into the enormous office. "Hello, Mr. Maxwell, I'm—"

I'm blindsided as familiar coffee-colored eyes meet mine. A man whom I thought I'd never see again is standing behind the desk. My one and only one-night stand—the man who rocked my world so thoroughly, I was sore for days. *That* guy is now apparently my new boss.

Fuck.

I can feel the color draining from my face as his eyes light up. "Ms. Jacobs, so nice to see you again. Is it okay if I call you Avery?" A sexy smirk slowly forms on his lips. "Or would you prefer *Angela*?"

I'll say it again: Fuuuuuck.

CHAPTER TEN

LIAM

I get an evil measure of satisfaction as shock transforms Avery's features.

"You...you said your name was Max," she sputters.

I walk to the front of my desk and lean back. "I did. Which was a lot closer to the truth than the name you gave me."

My dick gets hard—well, *harder*— when unadulterated fury paints her face. "Did you know? Did you know who I was that night?"

She worries her lip between her teeth as my eyes slowly travel the length of her body. Her long brown hair is pulled back, putting the slender column of her neck on display. She's wearing a fitted black blazer with a matching pencil skirt. Both showcase her curves perfectly, toeing the line between sexy and professional. As my gaze lands on her cherry red stilettos, naughty librarian fantasies flash through my head, causing me to smile.

"Are you referring to the night that I defiled your tight little body *four times*? Then, yes, I did know who you were."

Her mouth gapes, and it takes everything in me not to drop my pants and slide my dick into it. I fight back a groan as a memory surfaces of doing just that. Avery was so damn enthusiastic as her pouty lips bobbed up and down my shaft. She moaned when I shot my load down her throat, licking her lips afterward like it was the most delectable treat. Hands down the best blowjob of my life.

She glares at me, making the erection situation even worse. "Was that some sort of twisted interview for you? Is that why you offered me the job? Because I'll have you know, I do *not* mix business with pleasure. There's no way I'm sleeping with you again."

I bark out a laugh. "Hell, no. I didn't even know you had left Reed's company until the next morning. I offered you the job because you're one of the best in the business. And I'd hate to break it to you, but I have no trouble getting laid. I don't need to bribe anyone."

Avery straightens her spine. "This is never going to work unless we both agree to wipe the slate clean; act as if we've never met before today."

I give her a condescending smirk. "I don't know if I can do that, Ms. Jacobs." I walk toward her, against my better judgment, until her back is pressed against the door. Reaching behind her to turn the lock, I say, "But what I *do* know, is that you scream when I tongue your delicious cunt. I know that you're talented-as-fuck when giving head." I wrap her low ponytail around my fist and lean into her ear. "I also know that you *loved it* when I had my dick up your ass. In fact, I'd bet my Maserati that I'm the *only* man to ever have that particular pleasure. All in all, that night is pretty hard to forget, sweetheart." I press myself into her so she can feel how hard I am before stepping back with a wink.

Her face reddens. I can practically see the cartoonish steam bursting out of her ears. "You arrogant bastard!"

I brush imaginary lint off my suit jacket. "That may be, but you can't deny that I'm the best you've ever had. That it's *me* you think about every night as you're fingering yourself."

Avery scoffs. "You give yourself way too much credit. I've had better."

I raise my eyebrows. "Oh really?"

She parks a hand on her curvy hip. "Really. You're not nearly as great in bed as you seem to think you are."

Challenge accepted. "Is that so?"

Avery nods. "That's—"

I press my mouth against hers before she can feed me another lie. Her hands immediately begin working my belt loose while I shove her skirt up to her waist and slide her lace panties aside. I groan when I slip two fingers inside, feeling how fucking drenched she is.

I pump my fingers in and out. "Would you like to amend your previous statement?"

Avery finally gets my zipper down and shoves her hand into my pants, palming my engorged cock. "I like you much better when you don't talk."

I bite her earlobe. "Yet another lie. You fucking love how I talk to you. You wouldn't be this wet before I ever laid a finger on you if you didn't."

She gasps when I press the pad of my thumb

against her clit and begin moving it around in circles. "Just shut the hell up and make me come."

I remove my fingers, causing Avery to whimper in protest. I spin her around and lead her to the tufted leather couch against the wall. Placing my hand on the small of her back, I encourage her to lean over the arm of it until her perfect ass is pointed toward the sky. I roll her panties down to her knees and bite one heart-shaped cheek, causing her to yelp. Goddamn, she has a beautiful ass. As much as I want to take it right now, we don't have the time for that. Without another thought, I retrieve a condom from my wallet, slide it down my length, and enter Avery's warm, wet heat in one hard thrust.

I clap my hand over her mouth when she moans. "Unless you want everyone out there to know what we're doing, I suggest you keep quiet. Understand?"

She nods.

I slip my hand around her front, finding her swollen clit. Avery trembles beneath my touch, struggling to keep quiet as I show her no mercy. I'm not a fucking idiot; I know this can't happen again. But I am selfish enough to steal this moment and ruin her for all other men first.

Does that make me a prick? Maybe. Still doesn't change the facts.

"Oh, fuck...fuck...fuck!" she shout whispers.

"You've had better, my ass," I grumble as her pussy convulses around me.

With a few more thrusts, I'm coming, too, with a stifled cry into her shoulder. As soon as I've been milked dry, I step into my ensuite bathroom to get rid of the rubber and tuck myself back into my pants. Through the reflection in the mirror, I can see Avery smoothing down her skirt, looking around the room as if she's trying to figure out what the hell just happened.

Neither one of us says a word for a good minute. Finally, I step back into my office and say, "Don't worry though; I don't shit where I eat. I have no interest in *fucking* you again either, no matter how exceptional your pussy is. From here on out, this is strictly professional."

The rage is back on her face. "This," she gestures between us, "was a mistake. It will *never* happen again."

I quirk my head to the side. "Isn't that what I just said?"

Avery's fists clench by her side. "You're an asshole!"

"I thought we've covered that, too."

She throws her hands up in exasperation. "I can't work for you. I would've never accepted the job if I knew that *you* were Liam Maxwell."

I roll my eyes. "Which is exactly why I allowed Nick to take care of everything. Although, a simple Google search would've shown you exactly who I am. Quite frankly, I'm rather disappointed you didn't check me out before agreeing to move across the country."

Her jaw clenches. "Why would I? This company has a solid reputation and a lengthy list of A-list clients. It doesn't matter what my new boss looks like. It's about the job."

I nod. "I agree. Which is why you're going to forget the fact that we've fucked—five times now, in case you weren't keeping count—and do your job. Just like I'm going to do mine. You accepted my offer, Ms. Jacobs, because you knew you wouldn't find a better one. This is your chance to make an even bigger name for yourself and show that asshole he should've never fired you. Hopefully, all while making me a shit ton of money."

Avery glares at me. "I *resigned* from Reed & Associates."

I wave my hand dismissively. "Technically, yes.

But you and I both know that you didn't really have a choice." I hold my hand up when I see the outburst bubbling up her throat. "Before you say anything, I know that dickhead's accusations were false—you have too much integrity for that."

Her rage calms, but only slightly. "How do you know about that?"

I shrug. "I *may* have fucked the elder Reed's secretary a few months ago, and I *may* have alluded to a possible repeat in exchange for information."

"You're unbelievable," she mutters under her breath.

"We've already established that as well, when you were coming all over my dick." I wink.

Her cheeks redden. "This is not going to work if you keep bringing up our...mistake."

"Agreed." I unlock the door and swing it open. "On that note, welcome to Maxwell & Company. I know we'll do *incredible* things together."

Avery looks through the anteroom and breathes a sigh of relief when she sees that it's empty. She doesn't need to know that I had Olivia take a long lunch. Initially, it was because I didn't want anyone to hear the yelling that I was expecting once Avery learned who I was. It just happened to be a bonus that she was screaming my name for other reasons.

I almost laugh when she offers a handshake. "Thank you, Mr. *Max*well. I appreciate the opportunity."

My fingers hold on a little longer than necessary. "It's *my pleasure*, Ms. Jacobs."

I watch her hips sway as she leaves the room and my dick perks up in appreciation. Damn, maybe keeping it in my pants is going to be harder than I thought.

CHAPTER ELEVEN

2 MONTHS LATER

AVERY

Liam Maxwell is the biggest dickhead that I've ever met. Unfortunately, he *has* the biggest dick I've ever felt, and my body remembers that all too well. I think I've caught him staring at my ass on a few different occasions, but then he acts like an even bigger asshole, making me think I imagined the whole thing.

He's beyond arrogant, but also unbelievably sexy, and it drives me crazy. For the first time in my life, I actually feel like I have a healthy sex drive, possibly even overactive, and it's all due to him. Thankfully, except for my first day, he's given me almost complete autonomy, hardly acknowledging my existence, so it's slightly easier to ignore my inconvenient attraction.

"Why am I so drawn to him, Heather?" I groan. "My life would be much easier if he wasn't so pretty."

Her laughter rumbles through the phone. "Aves, you know I support you one-hundred-percent, but I'm actually glad you're feeling like this."

"What the hell? Why?"

"Because you've never been hung up on a man before," she explains. "You were with Stuart for seven years, and even in the beginning, you never talked about him this often. Every time I hear from you, it's, 'my asshole boss this'...or 'my asshole boss that.' Asshole or not, you're wildly attracted to him, and you can't get him off your mind."

"But why? I can't stand him."

"Maybe. But your body likes him an awful lot."

I gasp as I look at the time. "Oh, shit! I'm late for a meeting. I've gotta go. Talk to you later."

I rush to the conference room to find my team of publicists waiting for my arrival with the bane of my existence sitting at the head of the table.

"Nice of you to finally join us," he says. "Usually the person calling the meeting has the courtesy to show up on time." He looks at his watch pointedly. "I'm sure we would all like to get on with our day so let's get started, shall we?"

"Of course." I nod to my team of eight, ignoring the jerk up front. "My apologies for being late; I had a phone call run over. I've asked you in here to review our game plan for Finn Ryan's disastrous run-in with the paps."

Finn Ryan is one of Hollywood's biggest heartthrobs right now. He's gorgeous, incredibly talented, and philanthropic. The Irish accent doesn't hurt either. While he usually keeps his nose clean, he's got himself into a mess by causing a bit of a brawl. Finn punched a paparazzo that was getting too close to his wife. In a shark tank like that, once a single punch is thrown, all hell breaks loose.

Lydia, one of my publicists, raises a single finger. "I have an update. The guy that he punched has been discharged from the hospital. He has a fractured jaw and a mild concussion from banging his head when he crumpled to the ground. He's threatening to sue."

I roll my eyes. "Of course he is. Mr. Ryan's attorney is already on stand-by. I'll be making a statement to the press later this afternoon. Mr. Ryan will formally apologize for his actions, but I will be sure to emphasize that his intentions were honorable.

"His wife was going into labor with their twins. The guy that he punched was getting too close, blocking them from getting into their vehicle. When Mrs. Ryan got shoved in the process, almost falling face first to the ground, Finn stepped in to protect his wife and their unborn children.

"This idiot won't be suing once the media learns that he could've caused harm to the babies. Which by the way, mom and babies are doing just fine. They were born about an hour ago, slightly small since they're early, but they're healthy. I have a photographer from People scheduled a few days from now to showcase their happy family of four. The press will be eating out of our hands. Nobody can resist newborn babies."

Chuckles ring out throughout the room. I make the mistake of looking at my boss to find that he's still wearing his signature scowl. I swear that man has a stick permanently wedged up his ass.

"Any questions?" Liam asks.

My team all shake their heads.

"Very well, you're excused." Liam turns to me. "Except you, Ms. Jacobs. I'd like a word."

My eyes narrow. "Of course."

When my team leaves the room, he says, "Shut the door, Avery."

"Why? I have a press release to write. I don't have time to stroke your ego."

"Shut. The. Goddamn. Door," he growls.

I roll my eyes as I push it shut. "There. Happy?"

He mutters something that sounds suspiciously like, "I would be if you were riding my dick."

"What did you just say?"

Liam twirls a pen between his long fingers. The same fingers that played my body like a maestro. "I said, I will be if you get rid of this paparazzi prick. Finn Ryan has a twenty-million-dollar contract riding on the outcome of this mess. The studio doesn't want to deal with someone who has a temper. It's our job to make sure that he comes out of this squeaky clean."

I prop a hand on my hip. "At what point during the meeting did I give you the impression that it would end any other way?"

His eyes dart up quickly as if he had just been staring at my boobs. "Just don't fuck it up."

I glare at him. "I won't. Is that all?"

"A thank you would be nice."

"Don't hold your breath." I pause before walking out the door. "On second thought, go ahead. Since you'll run out of oxygen before I thank you for *anything*."

CHAPTER TWELVE

LIAM

I would've fired anyone else for talking to me the way Avery just did. She's blatantly insubordinate on a daily basis, but never in front of anyone else. She's the consummate professional unless she and I are alone together. When that happens, she's pure fire and sass, and my dick fucking loves it.

The sexual tension between us is ratcheting to an unbearable level. I promised myself that I wouldn't go there again—that her first day on the job was our way of working each other out of our systems—but that's apparently not the case. If anything, it's exacerbated the situation.

Every time I'm in my office, I think of her pliant body bent over my couch. I envision setting her on my desk, spreading her legs, and licking her from ass to clit. And when I'm jerking off in the shower, it's to the memory of her riding me, tits bouncing in front of my face. Fuck, I miss her tits. A button on her blouse came undone earlier, exposing a little glimpse of the curves that lay beneath. I couldn't stop staring at her chest, wishing I could suck her taut pink nipples into my mouth.

Christ, I'm fucked.

I groan as I adjust myself beneath the conference table. In all my thirty-five years, I've never met a woman who can push my buttons like Avery can. She's a raving bitch more often than not, but just the thought of her makes me hard. The woman loathes me, no doubt, but I obviously have the same effect on her. She *wants* me, whether she likes it or not. I'm not sure if she even realizes it, but her lips part anytime she looks at me like she's thinking about kissing me. Whenever she catches me staring at her ass, her nipples pebble through the silky blouses she favors. She crosses and uncrosses her legs to ease her throbbing center, whenever I'm even more of a prick than usual, as if my assholery excites her.

I've never been more attracted to a woman. Before she waltzed into my life, nothing and no one has ever caused me to lose focus. This business is my life, and I fucking hate her for being such a temptress. But then again, that just makes me want to redden her perfectly plump ass with my hand until she begs me to drive my cock into her. Mouth, pussy, ass—I'm not really particular since the end result is the same.

I rake my hands through my hair, trying to think about anything but Avery so I can walk out of here without tenting my slacks. When it takes a good twenty minutes of reciting sports stats in my head, I'm resolved on what I need to do. Plain and simple, I need to fuck someone else until my dick stops craving the one woman I can't have.

CHAPTER THIRTEEN

4 MONTHS LATER

AVERY

"So, you work in public relations, huh? I bet you meet lots of celebrities."

I slowly sip my dirty martini as I look my date over. He's a good-looking guy—about six feet, brown hair, brown eyes, and an athletic build. In short, he's exactly my type, but so far, he's boring as fuck.

"I do. Although it's not as glamorous as one might think. They're just normal people."

He laughs. "Yeah, normal people that cause messes you have to clean up."

I chuckle. "Right. So, what was it that you did again, Chad?"

"I'm a bartender," he replies. "But I'm trying to break into the acting biz."

Of course he is. This is L.A. after all.

I nod. "It's a tough business to get into."

"Yeah, much harder than I thought, for sure. I bet you know some casting agents and directors though."

"I've met a few here and there."

Chad flashes his pearly whites. "That's what I thought. So maybe if tonight goes well, you could pass my name along?"

I quirk my head to the side. "You want me to pass your name along for what, exactly?"

He digs a business card out of his wallet. On one side is a headshot, and the back has his contact information and a mini bio.

"You know, for jobs. In this city, you have to know someone to get your foot in the door. I figured you could be my someone."

I raise my eyebrows. "You did, huh?"

Is that why he asked me out? For my connections? What an ass!

Chad seems to sense my irritation, so he starts backpedaling. "Well, you know, just in passing. If you want to. Now, enough about me, tell me more about you. What do you like to do when you're not working, Avery?"

Ha! When am I *not* working? This is the first personal outing I've had since arriving in L.A. six months ago. If I'm not in the office or meeting with clients, I'm asleep. Heather finally talked me into trying online dating since, according to her, all busy professionals do it. It took some serious creativity to allow enough time in my schedule to make this date happen.

"I work a lot," I admit. "I don't get much time for anything else."

His gaze heats up as he places his hand on my knee. "Oh, I see. So, you're just looking to hook up then? If you're pressed for time, we can skip dinner and just head to my place."

Okay, as much of an opportunistic jerk as this guy is, I actually consider his offer. Maybe sex with him will scratch this damn itch that I can't seem to get rid of. It doesn't help that Liam was looking exceptionally fine today in his new Tom Ford suit and freshly cut hair.

"Um..." Before I can answer, my phone buzzes in my purse. "I'm sorry, I have to check this in case it's a client."

"Of course. Please do."

I retrieve my phone and see that the bastard himself has sent me a text. It's like he knew I was thinking about him or something. I frown when I read his message. He's demanding that I return to the office to discuss something that we've already gone over in great detail.

"It's my boss." I offer Chad an apologetic smile. "I'm sorry, but I need to take care of this real quick."

I've learned the hard way that when Liam Maxwell wants your attention, he won't take no for an answer. There's no sense in trying to ignore him. I sigh as I respond to his message, resigned to the fact that I'm about to be clam-jammed.

CHAPTER FOURTEEN

LIAM

Who the fuck is that? His eyes haven't left Avery's cleavage once. Are they on a date? Where did she find this douche?

"Liam," my date whines. "Are you listening to me?"

I look across the table and take in the blonde. What was her name again?

I look down at my phone. "Excuse me, I just received an urgent message from the office."

Blondie pouts. "Okay, I suppose I'll just order another drink."

I nod. "You do that. I'll be back in just a few."

I head down the hall toward the restrooms, which are thankfully located next to the bar area where Avery is sitting. It's been six months since she started working for me and each day gets harder and harder to resist her.

I haven't been able to seal the deal with another woman since the first time Avery and I fucked. Not that I haven't tried. I've met up with at least two dozen Tinder matches, but the bleached-blonde surgically enhanced women that I usually go for, have lost their appeal. The only time I even considered having sex with one of them was because I swiped right on a woman that bore an awfully close resemblance to Avery. Too bad she had to open her mouth and ruin it.

I'm so sexually frustrated, I feel like I'm about to implode. I know it's affecting my work which makes me livid. I've never been a laid-back boss— my business has grown exponentially because I have high standards. But I've always maintained the charm that I'm so well known for. Now, people go out of their way to avoid eye contact with me. Everyone *but* Avery, that is. She fights me tooth and nail over every-fucking-thing. And worst of all, I let her. *I look forward to it* because sparring with her makes my dick hard. It's like foreplay. Foreplay that ends tonight, one way or the other. I can't do this anymore.

I pull up Avery's number in my phone and send her a text.

Me: I need you back in the office tonight so we can discuss your action plan for improving McAllister's image.

She surreptitiously looks down when her phone vibrates. I can tell she's offering an apology as she fishes her phone out of her purse and types a reply.

Avery: We've already been over this. I have it handled.

Me: I disagree. There are some points that I'd like to discuss. Meet me in the office in 30 minutes.

She frowns as she reads the new message.

Avery: I'm sorry, but I'm on a date, and I've had a couple of drinks. I will see you in the morning.

Me: It wasn't a request, Ms. Jacobs. If you've been drinking, take a cab and use the company card to pay for it.

I can practically hear the litany of curse words running through her head. She shoves her phone into her purse, not bothering to reply. I smile victoriously as she gives the douche the brush off. I wait for her to exit the restaurant before returning to my date to do the same. I need to haul ass to get to the office before Avery.

"Is everything okay?" she asks as I return to our table. Seriously, what the fuck is her name?

I dig enough money out of my wallet to cover the bill and set it on the table. "No, actually. I need to head back into work. I'm sorry, but we'll have to do this another time."

She bites her lip, trying to look sexy. "Can't you spare ten minutes? You're the best match I've had in, like, a month and I really want to suck your cock. I don't mind doing it in the bathroom."

I don't even hesitate. "I'm sorry, I really have to go. Raincheck?"

Jesus, what the hell is wrong with me? I just turned down no-strings-attached head.

What's-her-name frowns. "Okay, then. Another time."

Yeah, not likely.

CHAPTER FIFTEEN

AVERY

I storm through Liam's office door, not bothering to knock. "This better be really important, Liam! I finally had a chance to take a night off, and you just ruined it."

He actually has the nerve to look smug, sitting behind his desk like a king holding court. "Tough shit, Avery. That's the nature of this business. Besides, we both know that your date would've left you feeling unsatisfied at the end of the evening, so why bother going through the motions?"

"What the hell is wrong with you? You are the biggest egomaniac I've ever met!"

He smiles. "It goes with the big dick."

I turn away and rush out of his office without

another word. That man is impossible to work with! I don't know if the pay is worth the shit I have to put up with anymore.

When I reach my office at the end of the hall, I go to slam the door shut behind me, but I don't get the chance because Liam is bursting through it.

His nostrils are flaring. "Don't ever walk away from me again."

I throw my purse on a nearby chair. "Don't speak to me like that and I won't." I look him directly in the eye. "I am damn good at what I do. *You know this*, Liam; it's why you hired me. Yet, lately, you've been treating me like a goddamn intern, hovering over everything I do. I won't tolerate it anymore."

Liam's jaw clenches. "That's because this is *my* fucking company, something you'd do well to remember. I know you're fucking spectacular at what you do. *Every fucking thing you do!* Do you think I'd put up with your bullshit otherwise? You're the most infuriating woman I've ever met."

"*I'm* infuriating?" I laugh. "That's rich, considering you're the most aggravating man on Earth."

Liam runs a hand over his jaw. "It's called sexual frustration, sweetheart."

"Right," I scoff. "You'd have to be abstinent to experience that."

Trust me, I know. For the first time in my life, I understand why people obsess about sex so much.

He rolls his lips. "Exactly. I haven't fucked anyone in over six months, and quite frankly, I'm done with this dry spell bullshit."

Wait...what? We last had sex six months ago. Could he possibly be referring to that?

I shake my head in disbelief. "Six months ago is when you and I...when we...you know."

He lifts an eyebrow. "Fucked over my couch?"

I slice my hand through the air. "Yeah...that. Are you honestly trying to tell me you haven't had sex with anyone since then?"

"That's exactly what I'm saying. Give the girl a prize."

"I don't understand. Why?"

Liam takes a step forward. "For the exact same reason you haven't."

"You don't know that," I sputter.

He smirks and takes another step. "Yes, I do. Because everyone else pales in comparison. You can't duplicate our chemistry." Another step. "Avery, I've tried. I've fucking tried like you wouldn't believe, because it would sure as hell be a lot less complicated." One final step and I'm pinned to my desk by his hard body. Liam runs his finger along my jaw, causing me to shiver. "See that? One innocent touch lights your body on fire."

"Does not," I lie.

His finger continues down my bare arm, leaving goosebumps in its wake.

He smiles when he sees the evidence of how much he affects me. "Why do we deny ourselves? We're consenting adults."

I narrow my eyes at him. "I can't stand you."

His eyes twinkle. "I'm not so fond of you either, but my dick hasn't gotten the memo."

I gasp when he starts trailing kisses down the nape of my neck. "What happened to not mixing business with pleasure?"

Liam groans as he palms my breasts through my clothing. "I know it's a fucked up situation, but I don't give a damn. I want you too badly."

His erection is pressed against my abdomen as his fingers slip beneath the hem of my dress. I moan against my will when he finds that I'm not wearing any underwear and plunges two fingers inside of me.

"Fuck," I pant.

He smirks as he pumps his fingers in and out.

"Have you been bare down here all night, Avery? The night we met you weren't wearing panties either. Were you going to fuck your date? Or did you take these off before you came into the office, knowing we'd be here alone?"

"Don't flatter yourself. I didn't want any panty lines." I claw at his belt buckle until I pull the strap free and unbutton his slacks. "Get your dick inside of me, Liam."

He releases a low chuckle. "I didn't hear you say the magic word."

I glare at him. "*Now.*"

"That works, too." Liam lifts me until my ass is balancing on the edge of my desk and thrusts into me without any hesitation.

He leans his forehead against mine and groans. "Shit. Need a condom."

I watch as he slides out slowly, his thick cock painted with my arousal. "Don't fucking go anywhere. I'm on the pill and safe."

He shoves back in. "Me too. The safe part." His fingertips bite into my hips when I lock my ankles behind his back, pulling him in even further. "Fuck, Avery. You feel amazing. So." Thrust. "Fucking." Thrust. "Good."

I brace my arms on the desk behind me. "You, too. Now stop talking. You're ruining it for me."

He makes a growly noise before making quick work of the ties on my wrap dress. Within seconds, each half falls to the side, exposing my skin to the cool air conditioning. Liam slides his hands up my ribs, over to my lace-covered breasts. His gaze never leaves mine as his thumbs brush back and forth over my peaked nipples. He pulls the bra cups down and immediately sucks one of the tight buds into his mouth, making me cry out from the pleasure-pain sensation.

He leans into my ear, continuing his unforgiving rhythm. "Do you know how many times I've imagined this? Fucking you on this desk? Or better yet, on mine? Driving into your pussy relentlessly, until all you could think about was my cock and how perfectly we fit together. How no one has ever fucked you like I do. *No one* knows your body like I do, Avery. Whether you like it or not."

"Stop talking," I whimper. "Your ego is killing the mood."

He gets a wolfish grin. "Make me."

My hands go to his hair, gripping it hard while I crash my mouth against his. Our kiss is not gentle—it's a power struggle full of tongues dueling, teeth clashing, and lip biting. I'm vaguely aware of things crashing to the floor, but mostly all I can focus on is Liam driving into me with so much delicious force, it feels like he might split me in two. I really hope no one else decides to stop in the office tonight because I couldn't hold back my screams if my life depended on it.

Liam rolls his thumb over my clit, alternating circular motions with a sharp pinch that sends me over the edge. Warmth spreads down my spine and between my legs until my entire body is quaking. Liam's teeth dig into my shoulder as his release rolls through him a few moments later. I'm limp and breathless and completely, utterly in awe.

I have no idea how long we were going at it; all I know is that it was the most profound sexual experience of my life. How can a man that I detest make me feel so incredible? I've never been a reckless person—hell, I've never had sex anywhere but a bed before I met Liam—but that's exactly how I feel when I'm with him. I want it all, consequences be damned.

Liam eyes me curiously. "Are you okay? I might've lost control for a bit there."

I laugh, which is no easy task with him still

inside of me. "The control freak has finally found his kryptonite, huh?"

He tilts his head to the side, pondering my question. "I suppose so." He brushes a lock of sweaty hair away from my face. "You didn't answer my question. Are you okay? I didn't hurt you, did I?"

I give him a soft smile, surprised by his sensitivity. "Only in the best way."

Liam sighs, seemingly relieved. "Good. Because I want to do that again." His dick stirs to life inside of me. "Right now, in fact, if you're up for it."

I clench my inner muscles and wink. "I'm definitely up for it. Impressive recovery, Mr. Maxwell."

He smirks. "I've been waiting six fucking months for this, Ms. Jacobs. I'm making up for lost time."

He starts moving slowly, his dick growing harder with each slippery slide. Before I know it, Liam's magical touch is taking me to new heights once again, vanquishing all cognitive thought.

CHAPTER SIXTEEN

LIAM

Throughout my entire adult life, I had never thought about a woman after having sex. On the rare occasion I did have a fuck buddy arrangement, not once had I looked forward to actually seeing them. Sure, I was excited about getting my dick sucked or screwing a woman against the wall, but I never thought about the actual person I'd be doing it with.

Maybe that makes me an asshole, but I'm pretty sure we've already established that.

I was so careful to never cross that line, and yet somehow, Avery Jacobs has fucking obliterated it. I feel more alive when she walks into a room and restless when she's not around. It's been a few weeks since that night in her office and rarely a day has gone by that we aren't tearing each other's clothes off the second the rest of my staff goes home.

I would live with my dick inside her 24/7 if I could. I can't stop replaying images of sinking into her body from behind. Her sitting on my face, writhing above me, panting my name. Rubbing the sting away from her ass when I spank her for making me feel so goddamn out of control. She invades my every waking thought and the majority of my dreams.

We've clearly set boundaries that whatever this is between us, only happens in this building, outside of regular business hours. And during those business hours, we're at each other's throats, just as we've been from the start. There are no dates, no pillow talk or meeting at each other's houses.

But here's my quandary: I want more. Merely the sight of her infuriates me because I don't like catching feelings, yet I find myself falling harder and harder every day. It's impossible not to. I've always been the one wielding power, yet this woman has pushed me into unfamiliar territory whether she realizes it or not.

I've woken up hard so many times after dreaming about her, that I'm actually considering modifying our arrangement. I haven't spent the night with a woman in over a decade, but I'm quickly learning that my workplace trysts with Avery aren't enough. I'm not sure how I would even approach the topic, let alone whether or not she'd actually go for it, but my aching cock will never forgive me if I don't try.

Speaking of the woman of the hour...

The door shuts quietly as she walks into my office. I quirk my head to the side when she turns the lock with a devious smile.

"May I help you, Ms. Jacobs?"

I try to maintain eye contact as she walks toward me, but it's no easy task with the way her hips are swaying.

"Olivia just left for lunch."

"And?" I raise an eyebrow. "That's usually what she does every day at noon."

Avery bites her lip as she continues her approach. "Right. Which means we have an hour."

"An hour for *what?*" I'm pretty sure I know where she's going with this, considering she just kneeled in front of me.

She scratches her fingernails down my thighs. "I couldn't wait for tonight."

I smirk as I lift my hips just enough so she can

pull my pants down. "Oh yeah? And what is it that you have in mind?"

Avery wraps her fist around my dick and strokes me from root to tip. "I think you know exactly what I have in mind, Liam."

"Why don't you tell me? Just so there's no room for confusion."

I groan when she pulls the head of my dick into her warm, wet mouth then slides all the way down until I'm tapping the back of her throat.

She releases me with a pop. "I want your dick in my mouth until you're close, then I want to ride you until we both explode."

My head falls back when she takes me in deep. "Fuck, Avery."

She moans as her head bobs up and down, tongue swirling with the perfect amount of teeth raking against my shaft. I have to shove my clenched fist against my mouth to stifle my groan when she cups my balls and tugs lightly.

Doing this in the middle of the day is irrespon-sible and dangerous, but I wouldn't stop unless the building was on fire. Even then, I would probably assess the severity of the blaze before breaking our connection.

I run my fingers through her hair and across the

indentation in her hollowed cheek. Avery increases the suction, and when her icy blue eyes look up at me under thick black lashes, I'm a goner. As amazing as this feels, I need to bury myself inside her sweet cunt more than anything right now.

I pull her into my lap, loving the fact that she's taken to wearing dresses or skirts every day. Knowing she does it for me, so it's easier to touch her, drives me wild. My hands snake beneath the fabric to find her pantyless and soaking wet. I line myself up with her entrance, and in one smooth motion, I'm balls deep inside of her.

Avery moans. "God, Liam. Why is it always so good?"

I run kisses along her neck as she rides me slowly. "I don't know. Nothing has ever felt better than being inside you. I don't ever want to stop."

She gasps when I flick the tip of my finger against her clit. "I hate admitting this, but me neither."

The pressure builds with each swivel of her hips and I know I'm not going to last much longer. I coat my fingers in her wetness and focus my attention on her pretty pink clit. Avery works me harder, our breaths ragged from the increased tempo.

"Shit...Liam...I'm going to come."

"I know, baby. Just hold on."

Her rhythm is choppy as she chases her release, so I plunge into her from below, never letting up on her sensitive bundle of nerves. Avery muffles a cry into my shoulder as her inner walls spasm around me, shivers course throughout her entire body. A few thrusts later, I'm nuzzled against her neck, muttering unintelligibly as bursts of cum explode from within me.

After our heartbeats return to normal, I lift my head to look at her. *Really* look at her. A sheen of sweat covers her skin, her lips are swollen, and her eyes look drunk. She's the most beautiful fucking thing I've ever seen, and I feel like the luckiest bastard on Earth being with her like this.

Avery runs her fingers through my beard and taps my temple. "What's going on in that head of yours?"

I've fallen completely head-over-heels in love with you.

I press my lips against hers before pulling back with a bite. "I was just wondering how an asshole like me managed to snag a babe like you."

She chuckles as she releases me from her body and stands. "It was a weak moment on my part."

I give her a wry look. "A few dozen weak moments at this point."

"Right." She's smiling softly as she adjusts her dress and smooths down her hair. After a quick visit to the attached bathroom, she jerks her thumb over her shoulder and says, "Well, I should get back out there. I don't want to be here when Olivia gets back."

I fasten my pants and walk her to the door. "Hey, what do you think about amending our arrangement?"

An adorable crease forms between her brows. "How so?"

I lean against the wall. "I think we should give sleepovers a try. I'm sick of waking up hard because of you then having to wait at least twelve hours to do something about it."

Avery smirks. "Why are you blaming me for your morning wood? Isn't that something that men normally have?"

I shake my head. "Not this bad. And it's your fault because more often than not, my subconscious likes to replay our encounter from the night before while I'm sleeping."

She releases a throaty chuckle. "That does sound like a dilemma." I don't like it when her expression sobers. "I'm not sure, Liam. How would that work? If we're not having sex, we're irritating the shit out of each other." She points a finger between us. "What we have is working. We get off then we go our separate ways."

Fuck. Who would've thought I'd be on this end of a conversation like this?

"Just think about it." I shrug. "We can do a trial run when we fly back to New York next week— share a hotel room. If it doesn't work out, no harm, no foul."

Avery bites her lip, and it takes every ounce of willpower I possess not to press my mouth to hers.

"Okay." She points a stern finger at me. "But I'm keeping my own room so I can leave if you're driving me crazy."

I laugh. "Honey, you'll be too busy coming all over my face to worry about anything else."

I don't miss the way her nipples perk up beneath the sheer fabric of her dress.

She opens the door and throws a glance over her shoulder. "We'll see about that, you cocky son of a bitch."

CHAPTER SEVENTEEN

AVERY

Every year, PR professionals gather 'round to discuss the latest news, analysis, platforms, and strategies that we need to utilize to bolster our clients' image. Over the last five years, Liam's former Director of PR for the L.A. branch has attended on his behalf.

This year, Liam's being honored on the 40 under 40 list—people who are known for redefining the role of communications, PR, and marketing—so he has to be here and engaged throughout the event. The official conference doesn't begin until tomorrow, but right now, we're attending the welcome cocktail party, much to Liam's dismay.

Liam leans down close to my ear. "This schmoozing stuff is bullshit."

I smile. "Schmoozing is what you do for a living."

"Yeah, because that's what I get paid to do," he grumbles. "Making small talk with a bunch of schmucks doesn't affect my bottom line. If anything, it's *preventing* me from making money because I have to be here socializing instead of actually working. I don't like doing things if I'm not getting paid."

My lips twitch. "Oh, I don't know...I can think of a few things that you *really* enjoy doing. Things that you're *very* good at, and you don't make a dime."

His eyes light up with mirth. "Ms. Jacobs, are you actually *flirting* with me?" Liam places his open palm against his chest dramatically. "Be still my heart!"

"Don't get too excited." I roll my eyes. "I didn't say I *enjoyed* doing those things with you."

"Don't make me kiss you in front of all these people and prove you wrong. I'm sure it will cause quite the uproar, but you should know by now how far I'm willing to go to make a point."

I glare at him. "You wouldn't."

Liam couldn't look any smugger if he tried. "Try me."

We're locked in a silent stare down for at least a minute before we're interrupted.

"Liam Maxwell!" Clint Roberts, the primary publicist for a major social media platform, slaps Liam on the back like they're best buds. "I haven't seen you in years! They had to bribe you with an award to get you to come to this thing, huh?"

Liam pastes a smile on his face, but it's obviously forced. "Clint, nice to see you." Liam nods in my direction. "Have you met my Director of PR, Avery Jacobs?"

Clint shakes my hand and says to my boobs, "Yes, of course. Avery was quite the star here in New York. Nice to see you again." *But I'd rather see you naked* is clearly implied in his tone. "So this guy dragged you out to the West Coast, did he? If you ever get tired of all those Hollywood types, there's always a spot for you on my team." *And in my bed*, is what he doesn't say.

I'm used to dealing with guys like this. Publicists are overconfident in general, but men like Clint take it to a new level. Not only is he arrogant as fuck, but he's also a misogynist. Lord knows I got enough of that working for Stuart's father.

Liam looks like he's about to punch this guy, so I offer a saccharine smile and say, "Thanks for the offer, Clint, but I'm quite happy at Maxwell." I lean into him conspiratorially and lower my voice. "Besides, you could never pay me enough to work for a prick like you."

Clint narrows his eyes. "I see your new boss is rubbing off on you." His gaze flicks to Liam. "If you'll excuse me, I see other people I'd rather chat with."

"Yeah, you do that," Liam mutters. When Clint is out of earshot, he turns to me. "You okay?"

"Why wouldn't I be?" I shrug.

"Because that guy is a dick," he replies. "And he wouldn't stop looking at you like you were the juiciest steak he'd ever seen."

"You're always a dick and look at me the same way."

"True, but you love it when I do it."

I laugh. "Always so full of yourself."

"I'd rather *you* were full of *me*. We should make that happen. Haven't we been here long enough?"

"We could make this faster if we split up," I suggest. "How about you cover the left half of the room, and I'll cover the right? I'll meet you upstairs in an hour."

Liam nods. "Make it forty-five minutes, and you have yourself a deal."

Forty minutes later—not that I'm counting—I'm about to duck out of the ballroom where the party is being held, but an all too familiar hand on my arm stops me in my tracks.

I recoil away from him. "Stuart, you lost the right to touch me ten months ago."

My ex-fiancé gives me a smarmy smile. "Aw, c'mon, Aves, don't be like that. I haven't seen you in forever."

"Also something you lost the right to when you lied to get me fired."

"I really thought it was you," he insists. "But afterward...I realized I was wrong and I'm sorry about that. I even told my father, but you were already in California."

I take a moment to look him over. How did I ever find this man attractive? Sure, he's handsome in a conventional sort of way, but beneath the surface, he's a venomous snake searching for any opportunity to strike. Why did I not see that?

I've obviously been staring too long because Stuart takes that as an invitation to get into my personal space. "I miss you, Aves. I miss *us*. You have a room upstairs, right? I'd really love to get...reacquainted."

I shrug off his unwanted touch, yet again. "What would Callista think about that, Stuart?"

He waves his hand dismissively. "Callista was a blip on the radar—an err in judgment, if you will. She couldn't hold a candle to you, Avery. No one can."

Can you believe the nerve on this guy? Right before I'm about to go off on him, a deep voice rumbles behind me.

"Avery, are you ready to go?" Liam places a proprietary hand on my lower back, which does not go unnoticed by Stuart.

"Yeah...sure," I say. "I was done with this conversation before it ever began." Liam puts a little pressure on my spine to lead me out of the room.

"Is that how it is now?" Stuart scoffs.

I halt. "Is that how *what* is, Stuart?"

He gestures to Liam and me. "You're sleeping with your boss? I guess that explains how you got such a big promotion. Although, Maxwell's standards are clearly low considering you're such a lousy lay."

What happened to *no one can hold a candle to you*? Before I have a chance to tell Stuart to fuck off, Liam has him pinned against the wall.

"Listen to me, you fucker," Liam growls. "First of all, Avery got the job because she is more talented than you will ever be. Hell, she's more talented than most people in this industry. You and I both know that she did all the work and you just went along for the ride."

Liam leans in closer and lowers his voice so only the three of us can hear. "Secondly, she is a *fantastic* fuck. Incredibly responsive. Enthusiastic. Willing to try *any*thing. She's so insatiable that she blows me under my desk on her lunch hour. I really want to strangle you right now, but I suppose I should be thanking you for screwing up." Liam steps back and straightens his tie. "She's the best fucking thing that's ever happened to my business or my dick."

Stuart's face is so red, it's turning purple. His eyes widen when he glances around the ballroom and sees how much attention we've drawn. Mine do the same. I want to throttle both men before me, but that would only cause a bigger scene. Instead, I calmly straighten my spine and walk out the doors without another word.

Liam's right behind me. "Avery, wait."

I whip around and pin him with a murderous glare. "I *will not* have this conversation right now. You've caused enough trouble. I can't be seen with you."

He adopts a casual stance. "Fine. I'll get a drink in the bar and meet you upstairs after."

"Fine," I huff.

I ignore the curious glances as I wait for the elevator. Once I'm inside my room, I kick my shoes off and pace back and forth, taking deep breaths. One thing's for sure: when Liam Maxwell steps through that door, he's going to get an earful.

CHAPTER EIGHTEEN

LIAM

In hindsight, attacking that douche wasn't the smartest move, but I couldn't let him get away with speaking to Avery like that. When I saw him standing next to her, with his hand on her arm, I didn't think; I reacted. Like a Neanderthal, at that.

I step into my hotel room and glance at the adjoining door. Avery had insisted on having her own room in case we drove each other crazy, but I wasn't going to let her get very far. I called the hotel immediately after she left my office that day to ensure we had connecting rooms.

Her side of the door is closed so I knock, preparing myself for her wrath. Is it wrong that my dick gets hard just thinking about seeing her all fired up?

After a few beats, she opens the door and steps aside so I can cross the threshold. A lesser man would've pissed his pants with the look she's giving me.

I pointedly glance at the bed. "You're obviously angry. We should probably just fuck it out of you. It'd be a shame to waste the opportunity to use a bed now that we finally have one in front of us."

She eyes the king-sized mattress before crossing the room and taking a seat at the desk. "The last thing I want to do right now is have sex."

I loosen my tie and unbutton the top two buttons of my shirt. "I didn't say anything about having sex. I said *fuck*—something you and I do very well, especially when we're mad."

Avery rolls her eyes. "You have no idea how precarious of a situation you've put me in, do you? You have no idea how your jealous boyfriend routine may have ruined my reputation."

"Jealous boyfriend, my ass," I mutter.

She bolts out of the chair and throws her hands up in exasperation. "Are you even listening to yourself, Liam? The way you behaved down there was unacceptable! Not only am I going to be the subject of every gossip ring in town, but now people are going to actually question my accomplishments. They're going to think I've screwed my way up the ladder!"

"That's fucking ridiculous," I scoff. "Anyone with half a brain can see how fucking smart and capable you are. I was defending you down there, Avery. You should be thanking me. Preferably with my dick in your ass but I'd accept your mouth, too."

"Are you fucking crazy? I don't want you anywhere near me." She slams her hands into my chest, trying to push me backward. "You're a goddamn narcissistic sociopath!"

I close my hands around her clenched fists when she tries shoving me again. "Watch your fucking mouth."

Avery struggles against my hold and stumbles backward when I release her. "Or what, Liam? What could you possibly do to me that would be any worse than what happened down in that ballroom? You fucking humiliated me!"

"Will you open your goddamn eyes?" I yell. "You're missing the point!"

"What point?" she screams.

"*That I fucking love you*! I can't stand you half the time, but somehow, I fell in love with you anyway." I take a deep breath and add, "He had his hands on you, Avery. *No one* touches what's mine. And. You. Are. Mine."

She blinks rapidly as if she's stunned. Then in the next moment, she launches herself at me and crashes her mouth against mine.

"I'm so pissed at you right now," Avery mumbles.

I bite her lower lip. "Yeah, well, I'm not so crazy about you right now either."

"Just shut up." She pulls my shirt out of my pants and starts undoing the buttons.

I fumble with the zipper on the back of her dress, then momentarily break our kiss so I can pull my shirt and tie over my head. Our desperation is unmatched—a kind so consuming, it wouldn't be satisfied until it caught fire and burned to the ground. We're a tornado of sloppy kisses and greedy hands as we undress each other. We laugh when our tangled limbs tumble to the floor in our haste until finally, we are blissfully skin to skin. It's no longer a laughing matter once her naked body is pressed against mine.

Instead of moving to the bed, I grab Avery's thighs and scoot my body down until her glistening pussy is right above my face. She gasps when my tongue darts out and finds her hot center, already swollen with arousal. I feast on her beautiful snatch until she's moaning loudly. I tilt her pelvis up so I can rim her ass while plunging my fingers into her cunt. I don't usually eat ass, but I can't seem to stop with her. Avery is so vocal, telling me how much she wants it—how much she loves this—I wouldn't be surprised if people two floors down could hear us.

This stunning woman is riding my face unabashedly, throwing around pleas like *more, harder, right there,* and *don't stop* until she's coming so hard *I* fucking see stars. Probably because her thighs are squeezing my head like the most exquisite vise. Once the tremors subside, I scoop her up, bend her over the edge of the mattress, and slam into her tight channel over and over as she claws the duvet, crying out in pleasure.

I lube my finger with her juices, spread her ass cheeks, and finger her puckered hole. Her back arches when I add a second digit. She pushes back into me eagerly, climbing higher and higher from being stretched so wide. As uptight as Avery seems on the surface, she's a fucking lioness in the sack.

My filthy girl *loves* double penetration.

I scissor my fingers in her tight hole. "I want your ass, Avery. Are you going to give it to me?"

"Yes! Yes! God, yes!" she screams as another orgasm rips through her body.

I pull my dick and fingers out as her muscles fall lax. "Don't move."

I run back into my room, going straight for my toiletry bag to grab the bottle of lube I brought with me. You never know when you might need it, and I'm a man who believes in always being prepared. I coat my dick with the slick gel, and stroke myself as I return next door. Avery's done just as I asked and hasn't moved a muscle. I trail a finger down her spine and spread her ass cheeks with my hands.

"You ready for me?"

She moans as I press the flared head against her tight little rosebud. "Stop screwing around and get your dick inside me."

Avery moans when I slap her pussy for having such a smart mouth. I press forward, and my cock easily slides into her tight little ass. I pinch her clit, easing the way to go farther and farther until my balls are touching her round cheeks.

We've done this several times now so I should know what to expect, but I can never seem to prepare myself for how tight she is.

I groan against her back. "Fuck."

"God, Liam," she pants. "Move, damn it."

"Give me a second."

I'm going to blow my load in two seconds if I move right now. She's wrapped around me so tightly, I actually worry she might cut off my circulation. Avery squirms as I tilt her forward even more so my fingers can toy with her pussy. She whimpers as I slide two fingers in and out, waiting until my dick calms down enough so I finally can move inside her ass.

Once I'm confident I won't embarrass myself, I begin a slow glide, in and out, matching the tempo with my fingers in her cunt. No more than two minutes later, her thighs are tensing again, signaling another impending orgasm. I know I won't last once she begins clenching around me, so I pick up the pace, shoving myself into both holes until she's shouting incoherently, gripping my cock and fingers so tightly, I couldn't pull out if I wanted to.

"Fuck...Liam...right there...don't stop!"

"Not going to happen, sweetheart," I grunt.

I thrust into her a few more times before my balls tighten and lightning shoots down my spine. I bite into her shoulder as I empty into her, progressively slowing my strokes until I've stilled completely. We both lie here as we catch our breath until I reluctantly withdraw and prompt her to flip over.

I crawl up the mattress beside Avery, smiling as I see her sleepy, sated expression. Wrapping my arms around her, I pull her into me and kiss her tenderly. We continue like that for a while before she pulls away with a sigh.

"What are we doing, Liam? What is this? What happens when we get back to L.A.?"

I press my forehead to hers. "I don't know. But I'm sick of pretending it's nothing. If we're going to do this, we're not going to hide it anymore. We'll just look guilty, and that's the last thing either one of us needs. I want more, Avery."

She studies me for a moment. "More?"

I run the bridge of my nose along the slender column of her neck. "Yes, *more*. More fucking, more sleepovers, more fighting, more everything."

She laughs. "*More fighting?* Don't you think we do that enough?"

I pull her flush against me so she can feel my growing erection. "Don't pretend you don't love it. You get off on it just as much as I do."

Her eyes dance with amusement. "I plead the fifth." She gasps when my hands wander below her waist. "Seriously, though, how are we going to fix what happened earlier tonight? I want more too, Liam, but not at the expense of my career. I've worked too hard to get where I am. I have to be a realist here. If people find out we're sleeping together, they're going to assume the worst."

"I'll fix this, Avery. After I'm done, nobody will dare accuse you of any wrongdoing."

She frowns. "How can you be so sure?"

"Because this is what I do. This is what I've made *billions of dollars* doing. I just need you to trust me, okay?"

Avery sighs. "Okay."

CHAPTER NINETEEN

AVERY

"Mmm, good morning, beautiful," Liam grumbles.

I stretch languidly as he presses his body into mine. Every muscle in my body aches in the most delightful way. I guess there's something to be said for sleepovers with him after the night we had.

I yawn. "It would be if some asshole didn't keep me up most of the night."

He chuckles into the back of my neck. "I'm not sorry." He grinds his erection into my backside. "Fuck, I love waking up with my dick nestled into this ass."

I moan when his hand snakes around my front and starts playing with my clit. I can feel myself getting wet, and I'd be embarrassed by how little effort it takes him, but I'm too busy appreciating the stretch when he thrusts into me from behind. This is a position we haven't really been able to enjoy at the office, so there's definitely something to be said about having sex in a bed. I love the way his muscular torso feels sliding against my back—how he hugs me close as he grinds into me, easily reaching my breasts or my slick flesh.

Something shifted between us last night. The push and pull is still there—I don't think we're capable of not inflaming each other's tempers, and truthfully, I wouldn't want that. But there's something else now...as if we've stripped back a few layers, exposing a tenderness that wasn't there before. We talked for hours—in between all the sex —and discovered that we have a surprising number of things in common.

I can't believe he dropped the L-bomb. We haven't addressed that elephant in the room yet— I'm still trying to process it, really. I know I have feelings for him, but is it love? All I know is that I've never been drawn to a man like I am to Liam.

Like he said last night, we drive each other crazy, but it's not necessarily a bad thing. I've never felt anything remotely close to this with another man, not even Stuart. With him, I think I was more indifferent than anything, as pathetic as that sounds. I never knew two people could have so much passion before I met Liam. And passion is something we have in spades, personally and professionally.

Liam and I take our time with each other's bodies, gentle touches punctuated by hard thrusts. Soothing kisses mixed with filthy words. My skin is on fire, yet goosebumps scatter across my flesh as an orgasm takes hold. Everything about this is so uniquely us. With every touch, every word, every kiss, we strengthen our connection.

When we're done, we shower together, get ready side by side, and head downstairs to face hundreds of our peers. I try quelling the sense of panic rising within me, but I'm not doing the best job. I'm certain Liam knows what he's doing, but the fact that he hasn't shared his plan with me makes me nervous. I thrive on control and willingly handing it over to someone else is not an easy task. Especially not when my future is on the line.

We're once again at the scene of the crime. The opening keynote speech will take place in the ballroom before we all break out into workshops for the day. Liam and I are scheduled for separate sessions to cover as much ground as possible so I won't see him again until the evening reception and award ceremony.

As expected, we're already surrounded by whispers and stares, though we both do an impressive job of appearing unconcerned. I always thought my game face was infallible, but Liam could definitely teach me a thing or two about remaining poised during a crisis. Well, except for last night which is why his outburst garnered so much attention.

We greet people in passing as we scan the place cards looking for our table. When we find it, Liam and I take our seats and make small talk with the other people at the table. The emcee announces that we'll begin shortly and asks the remaining stragglers to take their seats. Liam and I have already turned our attention to the makeshift stage at the front of the room, so we don't notice who filled the two empty chairs directly across from us until the slimy bastard speaks.

"This should be interesting," Stuart says, loud enough for everyone else at the table to hear. "Hopefully Maxwell can keep his hands to himself today and stay out of trouble."

Liam and I turn our heads quickly to face

Stuart and his father. Both men are wearing obvious contempt as they continue to take jabs.

Stuart's dad laughs. "I disagree, son. If he wants to throw away his empire for some temporary tail, he doesn't deserve it."

What an asshole!

I flash both men a glare, preparing to turn away and ignore them. Out of the corner of my eye, I can see Liam's fixed jaw and clenching fists. Damn it, this is the last thing we need.

I discreetly place my hand over his under the table. "It's not worth it, Liam. Ignore them."

Stuart Jr. smirks. "Yeah, *Liam*, you should probably take her advice. Since she seems to wear the pants in your little..." he waves his hand between Liam and me, "whatever it is."

There are six other people at our table watching our exchange with avid interest. So are the three full tables within earshot.

Liam directs his attention to Stuart Sr. and grins smugly. "Now, Reed, there's no need to be petty just because my third-quarter profits undoubtedly exceeded yours. I understand it must sting, knowing that my revenue growth is directly related to your loss, but that's life, right? You fuck up, you pay the price. I'm sure both you *and* your son can relate.

That said, we're all professionals here so let's act like it, shall we?"

Both Jr.'s and Sr.'s ears are red, their tell that they're fuming. When neither one has a rebuttal, Liam squeezes my knee and redirects his attention to the man at the podium. I cross my legs to ease the sudden ache, strangely aroused from that whole conversation.

As if he's reading my mind, Liam discreetly bumps his knee into mine and whispers, "Later."

The entire time we're listening to the keynote speaker, all I can think is *later* cannot get here soon enough.

CHAPTER TWENTY

LIAM

I've been on autopilot throughout the entire day. Whenever Avery is brought up in conversation, or if I see her in passing in between workshops, the itch to be inside of her overrides any rational thought. My dick is doing all of the thinking for me which has never happened when business is on the line. It's a good thing I can do this job in my sleep because people are eating out of my hands when I sing Avery's praises.

As angry and panicked as she was about this whole mess, I'm strangely carefree. I am *not* a happy-go-lucky man in general, so I have no clue what this woman is doing to me. If anyone was going to affect me this way, I suppose I can't be surprised that it's a brilliant, gorgeous, firecracker like Avery.

I've grown a highly successful PR business from the ground up. I excel at public speaking, yet I'm terrified about making my acceptance speech tonight because so much is riding on it. I asked Avery to have faith in me that I'd dispel any nasty rumors, and I've done that for the most part during my interactions with key players today. But to tie it all together, I need everyone attending this conference to hear what I have to say about her, including her.

Especially her.

As I enter the ballroom for the final event of the conference, I immediately spot her standing in a corner, surveying the room. She smiles radiantly as I approach which gives me hope about what I'm about to do.

I prop myself against the wall next to her. "How've your meetings been today?"

"Good for the most part. I really enjoyed the workshop on how to leverage Instagram and work around their algorithms. I need to set up a training schedule for our social media team as soon as we get back."

"Sounds good." I have to make a concerted

effort not to stare at her tits. "Are you still planning to meet up with your friend tonight?"

"Heather? Definitely. We're heading to *Blanc*. She says she needs a wingwoman."

I smile suggestively. "Ah, *Blanc*. Where it all began."

She smirks. "Well, tonight will have a slightly different outcome on my end."

I raise my eyebrow. "It'd better be an *entirely* different outcome on your end."

Avery laughs. "Oh, really? And if it isn't?"

I lean into her ear. "Did you miss the part where I claimed your ass last night? Literally and figuratively?"

She shakes her head in amusement. "Definitely didn't miss that part."

"Just remember that when you're getting hit on tonight. Because we both know that's going to happen."

Her lips curve into a soft smile. "I'll keep that in mind, Liam."

I adjust my cufflinks. "I'm meeting up with Nick. Maybe we'll head over there."

"I never pegged you as a possessive guy, before. Oh, how wrong I was."

I casually tuck my hands into my pockets. "You seem to bring out the caveman in me."

Avery's throaty laugh makes my dick perk up. "So I'm learning."

I tap her shoulder with mine. "You get wet when I behave like a Neanderthal. You love it when I lose control."

She side-eyes me. "Not when it results in you causing a scene in front of a bunch of our peers."

"That's been taken care of," I say dismissively. "Has anyone bothered you today?"

Avery takes a moment to think about it. "Earlier in the day, some people were whispering here and there, but now that you mention it...no, they haven't. What did you do?"

I grin. "You'll see."

CHAPTER TWENTY-ONE

AVERY

"And our last honoree tonight, Liam Maxwell of Maxwell & Company. Get up here, Liam."

I clap as Liam takes the stage and shakes the presenter's hand. I glance around the room as he takes his place at the podium. Unsurprisingly, he's commanding more attention than any of the previous honorees. He just has this presence about him that makes you pay attention.

"Thank you," he says as the applause dies down. "Ten years ago, I was a cocky twenty-five-year-old punk with impossible dreams." He smiles when the audience chuckles. "I had only been in PR two years at that point, but I was determined to become one of the big players. I started my firm with very little but quickly made big strides. I've been incredibly fortunate over the years to have employees that make me look good."

More laughter.

Liam focuses his attention on me. "The past decade has been wonderful, but my world truly changed about eight months ago. That's when I met Avery Jacobs."

He nods in my direction, causing everyone's eyes to follow. I can feel my face flushing, and there's not much I can do to stop it.

He clears his throat. "I had been following her career for years, but I never had the pleasure of meeting her in person until that night. And what a night it was." He smirks suggestively, making my face even hotter.

What the hell is he doing?

"I asked her to come out to L.A. and work for me," he continues. "I don't know what I did to become such a lucky bastard, but she accepted my offer. Since bringing Avery on board as my director, my profits have grown faster than the previous nine-and-a-half years. Anyone who knows Avery—which I think is a large majority of us—knows how truly talented she is in this field. I think it's fair to say she has a unique skill set; a true ability to make anyone look good." He grins. "Hell, she's managed to do the impossible and tame me, so that's gotta count for something, right?"

I slouch in my chair as more chuckles spread throughout the room.

Liam gestures to me. "As you can see, I'm embarrassing her so I should probably get to the point." He holds up his award. "I've never been good at sharing, but I owe part of this recognition to her. She's the best director I've ever had, and I'm honored to call her not only my partner in this business but also in life."

What in the actual hell?

"If I'm lucky, there will be two Maxwells behind the Maxwell & Company brand one day."

My mouth gapes. *Did he just announce to this entire room that he wants to marry me?*

"To Avery!" Liam says.

"To Avery!" my peers repeat.

I'm still in shock as he takes his seat next to me, so I don't see it coming until he's grabbing my face and pulling me into him. He kisses me in front of all these people, and for a moment, I get lost in it.

When I finally come to my senses, I pull back, but he doesn't release me.

My eyes widen. "Did that really just happen?"

"It did." He smiles. "The question is, how do you feel about it?"

I bite my lip, thinking about it for a moment. "I have conditions."

His eyes light up. "Is that so?"

"Yep," I reply in a serious tone.

Liam releases me and sits back in his chair, not giving a damn that the entire room is invested in this conversation.

"First of all, you have to stop being such a possessive ass."

He laughs. "I can work on that."

I hold up two fingers. "Secondly, if you think that's an acceptable proposal, you're out of your damn mind."

"Noted." He nods as a grin spreads across his face.

"Third, *if* you ever figure out how to propose properly, I'm hyphenating my last name. You good with that?"

His hands cup my cheeks again. "Baby, I'm fucking *great* with that."

As he slams his lips against mine again, I don't even care that the room is erupting in applause. I kiss him back with everything I have, knowing without a doubt, that I'll be happily kissing this man for the rest of my life.

ALSO BY LAURA LEE

Dealing With Love Series (Interconnected standalones)

♥Deal Breakers (Devyn & Riley's story)

♥Deal Takers (Rainey & Brody's story)

♥Deal Makers (Charlotte and Drew's story)

Bedding the Billionaire Series (Interconnected standalones)

♥Billionaire Bosshole

♥Billionaire Bossman (Formerly Public Relations)

♥Billionaire Bad Boy (Formerly Sweet Temptations)

Windsor Academy Series (Books 1-3 must be read in order)

♥Wicked Liars

♥Ruthless Kings

♥Fallen Heirs

♥Broken Playboy (Bentley's story-can be read as a standalone)

Standalone Novels

♥Beautifully Broken

♥Happy New You

♥Redemption

If you'd like to be one of the first to know about new releases or sales, sign up for Laura's newsletter at:

https://www.subscribepage.com/LauraLeeBooks

ABOUT THE AUTHOR

Laura Lee is the *USA Today* bestselling author of steamy and sometimes ridiculously funny romance. She won her first writing contest at the ripe old age of nine, earning a trip to the state capital to showcase her manuscript. Thankfully for her, those early works will never see the light of day again!

Laura lives in the Pacific Northwest with her wonderful husband, two beautiful children, and three of the most poorly behaved cats in existence. She likes her fruit smoothies filled with rum, her cupboards stocked with Cadbury's chocolate, and her music turned up loud. When she's not chasing the kids around, writing, or watching HGTV, she's reading anything she can get her hands on. She's a sucker for spicy romances, especially those that can make her laugh!

For more information about the author, check out her website at: www.LauraLeeBooks.com

You can also find her "working" on social media quite frequently.

Facebook: @LauraLeeBooks1

Instagram: @LauraLeeBooks

Twitter: @LauraLeeBooks

Verve Romance: @LauraLeeBooks

Reader's Group: Laura Lee's Lounge

TikTok: @AuthorLauraLee

ACKNOWLEDGMENTS

To my husband, Tad: You're my biggest supporter, my best friend, and my partner in crime. I love you 3000.

To my children, Kaitlynn and Carter: Thank you for not fighting too much while I was locked away trying to meet this deadline. You two are my greatest gift even when you're testing my sanity.

To my lovely betas Heather and Crystal: Thank you for being the first people to read Avery and Liam's story. Your feedback was invaluable.

To all the seriously awesome bloggers in the book world: I appreciate you more than words can ever say, as a reader and a writer. Thank you for all you do to help others find new book boyfriends.

To my ARC team and Loungers: Thank you for being such awesome, hilarious, and supportive ladies. Keep those Chris Hemsworth pics and GIFs coming!

To my editor, Erin Potter: Thank you once again, for polishing my work and making the final product so much better!

To Julia, Marika, Heather, Sylvie, Elizabeth, Ceri, Krista, Brenda, Susannah, Molly, and Stephanie: I cherish our group chats more than words could ever say. I love how well our collective brains can turn a perfectly innocent conversation into something wildly inappropriate. You never fail to make me smile even when I'm in a funk. I'm honored to have you in my tribe. I threw in some extra butt stuff just for you. ;-)

Last but never least, to my readers: I love sharing all the random shit that comes out of my brain with you. It's a privilege bringing stories into your life for a living.

Printed in Great Britain
by Amazon

40835370R00076